Gabrielle and Selena

Gabrielle and Selena

Peter Desbarats

Pictures by Nancy Grossman

Harcourt, Brace & World, Inc., New York

H

Gabrielle and Selena

7024549

GABRIELLE AND SELENA went everywhere together. They did everything together. Although they had lived in the world for eight long years, neither of them could remember a time when they had not been together. They were like sisters.

Gabrielle seemed to know what Selena was thinking; and sometimes Selena would know what Gabrielle was going to say even before she said it. If Gabrielle started to say, "Why don't we ask your mother for some...?" Selena would shout, "...ice cream!"

Gabrielle had long hair that was almost blond. She had hazel eyes, gray and green, like the eyes of a tabby kitten. Often she was quiet, as if she were dreaming about something or looking at something far away that no one else could see. But she wasn't *always* quiet.

Selena had short black hair. She had large brown

eyes. If you took a bowl made of dark wood and filled it with rainwater, that was the color of Selena's eyes.

Selena could do many things, but the thing she did best and most often was laughing. When she laughed, everyone else laughed too and felt happy.

But *sometimes* she was quiet.

One summer day, when they were sitting on Mr. Mayer's front steps, halfway between Gabrielle's house and Selena's house, Gabrielle said, "Sometimes I wish, Selena, that I were you."

"Why do you want to be me?" asked Selena.

Gabrielle put her chin on her hands. "I'm tired of being myself," she said. "Every morning I wake up in the same room, look at the same sister, say hello to the same father and mother, brush the same teeth with the same toothbrush, eat the same breakfast and read the same newspaper and..."

Selena looked at Gabrielle and said, "You don't read the newspaper."

"Sure I do," said Gabrielle. "I read it every morning, just like my father does."

"What did you read about this morning?" asked Selena.

"I was in a hurry this morning, and I didn't have time," said Gabrielle. "Anyway, every day I do all these same things, and I'm tired of them. I think it would be more interesting to live at your house."

"But it's the same at my house," said Selena. "I always wake up in the same room and look at the same brother and eat the same breakfast and drink the same coffee and..."

"You don't drink coffee," said Gabrielle.

"Sure I do," said Selena.

"This morning?" asked Gabrielle.

"I was in a hurry this morning and didn't have time," said Selena. "Anyway, I do almost the same things that you do every day."

"But you don't do them *exactly* the same," said Gabrielle. "It would be much more fun if I could be you and you could be me."

"That's silly," said Selena.

"No it isn't—it's magic," said Gabrielle. "All we have to do is put our hands together, like this, and put our feet together, and put our noses together, and I'll look into your eyes, like this, and..."

Selena started to laugh. "Your eyes look funny," she said. "They look like one big eye in the middle of your forehead."

"Stop fooling or it won't work," said Gabrielle. "Now we turn around once, and I say—'I am Selena.'"

"And I say—'I am Gabrielle,'" said Selena.

They each took two steps backward and looked at each other.

"Hello, Gabrielle," said Gabrielle.

"Hello, Selena," said Selena.

"Well," said Gabrielle, "it's almost time for supper. I'd better hurry. Good-by, Gabrielle. Have fun at my house. I mean, *your* house."

"Good-by, Selena," said Selena. "Don't forget to feed my cat. I mean, *your* cat."

When Gabrielle reached Selena's house, she rang the doorbell. Selena's mother opened the door and said, "Hello, Gabrielle."

"I'm not Gabrielle," said Gabrielle. "I'm Selena."

"Oh, I see," said Selena's mother. "Well, Selena, I don't understand why you rang the doorbell. Selena always just walks into the house."

"I forgot," said Gabrielle, and she walked into the house.

Selena's little brother was lying on the floor in the living room, looking at a book. "Hello, Gabrielle," he said.

"I'm Selena," said Gabrielle.

"OK," he said. "But you sure look like Gabrielle, Selena."

Selena's mother came into the living room. "Wash your hands, Selena," she said. "It's time for supper. And we're having your favorite vegetable—turnips."

"Turnips are my favorite vegetable?" asked Gabrielle, who couldn't stand them.

"Certainly they are," said Selena's mother. "You always have two helpings."

"Ugh!" said Gabrielle to herself.

When Selena reached Gabrielle's house, she walked right in. She went into the kitchen, where Gabrielle's mother was standing in front of the stove, and said, "What's for supper?"

"Oh," said Gabrielle's mother, "are you staying for supper, Selena?"

"Of course I am," said Selena, "and my name's Gabrielle."

Gabrielle's mother turned around and looked at her. "Where's Gabrielle? I mean, where's Selena?" she asked.

"Selena's at my house," said Selena. "I mean, *her* house."

"Very well, Gabrielle," said Gabrielle's mother. "Wash your hands for supper. We're having your favorite—a great big omelet."

"That's my favorite?" asked Selena.

"I always give you an extra-big helping, and you always come back for more," said Gabrielle's mother.

"Ugh!" said Selena to herself, because if there was one thing she couldn't stand, it was an omelet. She didn't like boiled eggs, scrambled eggs, fried eggs, or

poached eggs, and an omelet was about the most horrible thing you could turn an egg into. It tasted like wet newspaper to Selena.

Somehow Selena managed to eat most of her supper. When it was time for dessert, there was chocolate cake for Gabrielle's mother and Gabrielle's father and Gabrielle's little sister—who kept calling her Selena—and bread and butter for Selena.

"Where's my cake?" said Selena.

"Why, Gabrielle, you know you never eat cake," said Gabrielle's mother. "You always say that the best dessert in the world is bread and butter."

"I do?" said Selena.

When Gabrielle had finished most of her turnip, trying to look as if she liked it, Selena's father said, "Now it's time to clear the table and do the dishes, Selena."

"But I haven't had any dessert," complained Gabrielle.

"Why, you know we always have chocolate ice cream for dessert on Thursday, and you don't eat chocolate ice cream," said Selena's father just as a large helping was put in front of him.

"I don't?" said Gabrielle.

"Never!" said Selena's father. "You haven't eaten chocolate ice cream since your last birthday party, when it made you sick."

"Maybe I'd like it now," said Gabrielle. "Maybe I could try a little bit."

"I don't think that's a very good idea," said Selena's father, putting a huge spoonful of chocolate ice cream into his mouth. "If it made you sick, you couldn't wash the dishes."

"Wash the dishes?" said Gabrielle in a small voice. "But I always watch television after supper."

"I don't know what you're talking about, Selena," said Selena's mother. "You never watch television. You always say it's much more fun to wash the dishes."

At Gabrielle's house, Selena was sweeping the kitchen floor. Gabrielle's mother had said that this was what she did every night before she went to bed at seven-thirty.

"You mean *I* have to go to bed at seven-thirty?" asked Selena.

"Good heavens, you don't *have* to, you *want* to," said Gabrielle's mother. "Every time I ask you to watch television with me, you say that it's much healthier to go to bed early."

"Well!" said Selena to herself. "No wonder Gabrielle wanted to be me. Omelets. Sweeping the kitchen. Going to bed at seven-thirty. No television. This is a terrible way to live."

Then she looked up at Gabrielle's mother and said, "I'm going home."

"All right, Selena," said Gabrielle's mother, laughing.

At Selena's house, Gabrielle had just finished the dishes when Selena's father said, "Time for bed, Selena."

"But it's only seven-thirty," said Gabrielle.

"Is it that late?" said Selena's father. "My goodness, by this time you're usually sound asleep on the back porch."

"The *back porch?*" said Gabrielle.

"You always say that it's healthy to sleep outside," said Selena's father.

"But it's dark out there, and cold," said Gabrielle.

"I know," said Selena's father, "but that's the way you like it. I don't know how many times you've said that you'd rather sleep on the cold back porch and look at the stars than be warm and cosy in an ordinary bedroom."

"Boy!" said Gabrielle to herself. "I never realized that Selena was such a nut. Turnips. Washing the dishes. Sleeping on the back porch."

Gabrielle looked up at Selena's father and said, "I'm going home."

"All right," said Selena's father, smiling. "Good night, Gabrielle."

Gabrielle and Selena met on the sidewalk under the streetlight in front of Mr. Mayer's house.

"Hello, Selena," said Selena, looking at Gabrielle.

"Never mind calling me Selena," said Gabrielle. "I wouldn't be you for all the money in the world. You didn't tell me that turnips were your favorite vegetable."

"*Turnips*?" said Selena. "I can't stand turnips. But you didn't tell me that you loved omelets."

"Ugh!" said Gabrielle. "I hate omelets almost as much as I hate washing dishes."

"But you sweep the kitchen floor every night," said Selena.

"I do not," said Gabrielle, "and at least I don't sleep on the back porch."

"Who sleeps on the back porch?" cried Selena.

"But your father said..." said Gabrielle.

"And your mother said..." said Selena.

Suddenly the two little girls looked at each other and started to laugh. And their laughter sounded in the night like silver bells beneath the streetlights beneath the stars beneath the soft black sky.